For my super-kind and ever-so-clever
friends Mags and Manoëlle

This edition published in 2018
First published in 2014 by Scholastic Children's Books
Euston House, 24 Eversholt Street
London NW1 1DB
a division of Scholastic Ltd
www.scholastic.co.uk
London ~ New York ~ Toronto ~ Sydney ~ Auckland
Mexico City ~ New Delhi ~ Hong Kong

Text and Illustrations copyright © 2014 Sarah McIntyre

ISBN 978 1407 18543 9

THERE'S A SHARK IN THE BATH

BY SARAH McINTYRE

One morning, Dulcie noticed that Dad had
forgotten to let out the water from last night's bath.
The tub was full of cold, soapy, dirty froth.

But she saw
something else, too...

A

fin.

Dulcie hollered,

"There's a

SHARK

in the bath!"

Dulcie's mum just smiled. "Next you'll tell us there's an elephant in your cereal." "No — that would be silly," said Dulcie.

Dad rolled his eyes, "Well, you'd better go and fish out that shark, then."

So Dulcie did fish it out.

Pop!

Pop!
Up came
Mama Shark.

Pop!
Up came
Baby Shark.

Dulcie took a step back.
"Are you going to eat me?"

"OF COURSE!"
said Papa Shark.
"It's breakfast time!"
said Mama Shark.
"Pass me the ketchup!"
said Baby Shark.

But then Baby Shark looked around.
"Before we eat you, pleeeease,
can you tell me... **what is this?**"

"That's **toothpaste**," said Dulcie.
Then she had an idea...

Dulcie smiled. "We need toothpaste to play the Brushety-Brush Game!

And you have SOOOOO many teeth, you'll love it. Hup hup! Let's get busy!"

Say, "Aaaaaaaah!" ordered Dulcie.

"AAAAAAH,"
said Baby Shark.

Brush
Brush...

...Brushety-brush!

All three sharks were shrieking with laughter.

Then Papa Shark said, "AND NOW I THINK...

...IT'S TIME TO EAT YOU!"

Dulcie stomped her feet. "But you've just cleaned your teeth!" Mama Shark said, "Is that a problem? I think not." Baby Shark said, "My tummy's rumbling."

Dulcie shook her head, "Wait... before you eat me,
let's play the **Wiggety-Wig Game!**
I'll show you how." And she gave the pink
bottle a squeeze.

Splurt!

Now, if there's one thing a shark loves, it's **bubbles**.

Big **bubbles**,

small bubbles,

so many bubbles.

"Look at you!"

"LOOK AT ME!"

"NO, look at me!"

Then Papa Shark
clacked his teeth
and said...

"NOW IT'S TIME TO EAT YOU."
And Mama Shark said, "Yes, being this stylish is making me hungry!"
And Baby Shark said,
"Yummy yum, yum!"

"But wait!" said Dulcie.
"You haven't yet played the
Happy-Wrappy-Uppie Game.
Go on, pull the toilet paper!"

"Pleeeease, can I play?"
begged Baby Shark.
"Just one more game,"
said Mama Shark.
Papa Shark snorted,
"OK, BUT HURRY UP, KID."

So the sharks pulled and pulled and pulled the toilet paper and...

...oopsie-whoopsie,
oh my,
What a tangle!

Suddenly they heard a "knock knock" on the door...

...and everyone went quiet.

Dad boomed, "Is everything **all right** in there?"

"No problems at all!" called Dulcie.

"That's good," said Dad. "One more minute, then I'm **coming in**. If it's messy in there, you'll be in **trouble**."

Baby Shark whispered,
"Who's that?"

"That's my dad,"
said Dulcie.

The sharks whimpered. "Help! We don't want any trouble."
Dulcie gave them a stern look. "I will let you loose but only
if you help me play the Spick-and-Spanny Game."

So...

Splish,

Splash,

Splosh!

Together they cleaned that bathroom lickety-split!

Just then, the door handle began to turn...

Dad was coming in!

Papa Shark roared, "BACK TO THE SEA!"

The door swung open.
Dulcie stood there, grinning.
"I'm all finished in here!"
Dad huffed, "That's
such a relief."

Back downstairs, Dulcie's mother gave her a look.
"Now don't start playing with your food."
"Of course not," said Dulcie.

As Dulcie settled down to eat a nice, quiet breakfast, she heard a little rustle in her cereal bowl...

FIN